M000303687

Lucas and The Time-Traveling Fog

Benjamin Vena

TABLE OF CONTENTS

Chapter 1

The Journey Begins

Hello, my name is Lucas Robinson, and I'm a senior at Lincoln South Highschool in Hawkesville, Illinois.

You know how teachers would always say that, "this is your final year of high school, so make the most of it," "this is your final year to find out who you are," blah blah blah!

Well, I never really cared about questioning or listening to their talk, to be honest, and probably never will because I think it's a waste of time and energy for teachers to talk to me about finding my path in life. Plus, I don't want them to tell me how to live my life. They would always say to me that I shouldn't have any regrets in life unless I look back and reflect on the mistakes I made, and "that's the only way to look forward."

Like seriously, why talk about the past when we need to focus on the future? The future is the key to success in the world. If you can envision your future, you can prepare yourself to become rich. I always thought that my teachers don't know me at all, so why should I care? I can't possibly change my past, let alone someone else's, because once it is done, it's done. There's nothing you can do to change that.

It wasn't until my first day of senior year of high school that I changed my perspective on past events. You know the old saying, "Try walking in someone else's shoes." I was in someone's shoe; not just their shoes, but their whole body. First, let's get one thing straight about time travel. It's not like you see in the movies. You know, with a time machine or special car or something. But to be fair, I don't remember well how I traveled back to 1959 or even why. But it happened.

I always thought time travel would be like being in a long dream, but it wasn't like that at all. It's so exhausting to talk about it, but hopefully, letting you into my adventure through time will bring back some clues and answers on what I will be in life! Still to this day, I don't understand why time chose me of all people! Me! A blonde-headed, social media crazed, immature high school kid!

So, this is how the trip through time all went down.

Chapter 2

Senior Year

This all started on my first day of Senior year in Highschool on August 21st, 2019. I was your typical teenager in every way. I was always on my phone, always keeping up with the trends... my highest streak on Snapchat was 405. Can you beat that? Most importantly, I loved hanging out with my friends and family without a care in the world. I thought nothing could surprise me because I had been through it all. But I was in for the biggest and scariest surprise of my life, and I didn't even know it just yet.

My first day started out normal, to say the least, for the first day of school. I woke up from my bed, took a quick shower, dried myself, then got dressed and headed downstairs to make myself some breakfast. As I was preparing some waffles, I looked outside the kitchen window, and I noticed a lot more fog out than usual. But then again, that really wasn't unusual because I live in the southern part of Illinois, where it's typical to drive to school with your headlights on almost every morning.

I didn't think too much about it either, so I just went about my business as usual. Just as I was about to walk out the front door, my mom stopped me.

"Wait! Lucas, you forgot Grandpa's letterman jacket."

Now, this letterman jacket, from what I was told, was worn by my grandfather. He was like the coolest dude ever! His life was legendary. He often went to drag races in his youth, was the star quarterback back in his high school days, and was also kind of a ladies' man in high school.

My mom always said that he and I have a lot in common. My guess is because he was a very outgoing person like me and was friends with almost everyone. But as a grown-up, my grandfather was known around this small town as an honest and hardworking family man. He was a legend in my book, who I seriously idolized. To me, he was Superman.

Sadly, I... uh *cough* never had a chance to meet him because he died a few months after I was born. I've heard stories about his life and seen so many pictures, thanks to my grandmother Janet. Since I was little, she would always tell me the craziest adventures that she had with my grandfather. Man, what a life he must have had. I just wish I could spend time with him and get to know the real man. I think he and I would have great memories together.

Anyway, I thanked my mom for reminding me, grabbed the letterman jacket, and before I did anything else, I put it on with pride. Then I got into my car to begin the long 10-minute drive through this thick fog to school. I first plugged in my phone and turned on my favorite playlist, and backed out the driveway.

Everything...even the drive to school...was fine. That was until my phone decided to go dead! I first thought that my phone cord disconnected, but it was still plugged in. I tried a couple of times, hitting the power button to make it work again, but nothing happened. So, I unplugged it and tossed it somewhere in the backseat out of frustration.

Then out of nowhere, this green fog surrounded my car. I was hoping that I wouldn't be late on the first day, but in the back of my mind, I really wanted school to be canceled by this strange weather so I could get back and enjoy playing Fortnite with my friends and savor my summer just a little bit longer.

But in the meantime, I just had to keep on ahead and continued to drive with both headlights and hazards on at the same time, but this fog was getting so thick that it even made them useless! I was starting to get worried, and my ideas to try and see the road again were running out fast. I didn't even know if I was on the road at this point! It just seemed like never-ending waves of this green smoke!

I was bored out of my mind as I kept driving. I decided to put the pedal forward and just look at my car radio time, hoping it would change, but I noticed that it had also ceased working. It stopped at the same time as my phone, which apparently was 7:45 a.m., just five minutes before I made it to school. I then just stared at the emptiness of a nonexistent road to hopefully pass the time.

But this fog started to become thicker and greener because now, I could barely see my car, and all I could see was this stupid, thick green fog! All of a sudden, I heard this loud bang! It made me jump in my seat! I said to myself, "Oh great, lightning. Just what I needed right now." As soon as I said that, I heard a loud screeching metal noise that felt like it was coming from both inside and outside the car. It was so fast and painful that it literally made me scream, all the while trying to keep my car from flipping over and somehow stay on the road from this terrible storm!

While trying my best to keep the car hopefully on the road, I finally noticed a bright light shining through the fog that was ahead of me, and I could faintly see people in this distance. "Ha! Nothing can stop me now!" As I headed into this bright light, I immediately saw the school parking lot, and I looked behind me to see if the fog was still there, but to my surprise, there was no fog at all, and all the noise had suddenly stopped!

When I parked in the empty school parking lot and looked around, I saw that there hadn't been any rain or lightning in like forever! That threw me off-guard a little bit because I clearly remember hearing lightning strikes outside just moments ago.

Also, I saw people walking, sitting, and talking to one another. Like, just talking. Nobody was looking at their phone. In fact, nobody had a phone in their hand! I was so dazed and confused, like what did I just get myself into here? Finally, I saw people that

I hoped were girls walking to school in a poodle skirt. For real, who are these people?

Then came the school...Oh Yes, school! Which looked so different. I said to myself, "this can't be my school, can it?" I convinced myself that it was and maybe was just remodeled during the summertime without me knowing. I then had the courage to look around the inside of my car instead of being glued to the window to see what else had changed. Everything in my car was completely different. Seriously, I noticed that my seats looked interiorly different, almost as if it were the 1950s again.

"That's strange, but there's got to be something else. I just know there is!" I muttered. So, I checked under my seat and even the car air conditioning to make sure that what I was seeing was indeed real. All seemed normal, to say the least, but I still wasn't convinced that everything was fine. So, in a moment of panic, I said, "I know it must be the windows!"

I looked at all of my windows to see if they were cracked or broken, but to my surprise, they were perfectly fine, so that tossed the bird-hitting-my-window scenario out of the question. I thought maybe something or somebody hit my car! Maybe I hit them? Without any hesitation, I turned my car off and put my keys in my pocket. And as soon as I got out of the car and walked around the entire vehicle, to my amazement, it wasn't hit or hit anything at all. But it did change.

I rubbed my eyes to make sure that this was the same car that I drove through the fog, but nope, my 2014 Chevy Impala had changed to a 1959 Chevy Impala. How. How did this happen? Man, that's one cool ride! But this can't be my car? Can it? I wondered to my astonishment. So, to make sure that it was,I put my hand in my pocket to check my keys, but what came out was a ring full of keys that I'd never seen before in my life.

So, if this is my car, where did my actual car keys go, and how do I get in without my remote? I thought to myself. *It can't be as easy opening the door, right?* I tried to open the door, but it was obviously locked.

Wait a second; I have tried this before. I then remembered that I had, and it was during the summer when my friends and I went to a car show downtown Chicago, and when they were looking at other old rides, I went the opposite direction and stumbled upon this gorgeous red 55' Chevy bel Air.

The owner of this car was some old man, and he got up from his lawn chair and decided to test me by asking, "Hey kid, do you think you can open my 55 Bel-Air?"

"Ya, sure. Where's the remote?" I asked.

The old man laughed at my face and said, "No remote...son, just the key." "What! ... no way!"

He stated, "Look, I'll show you. See, old cars like this don't need remotes, just a basic key... see," as he unlocked the car. "Now, you try!"

I tried to open it using the key, and bam, it worked like magic. I thanked him for showing me, but before I left, he said, "If you ever buy an old car like this one day, you'll remember now how to lock and unlock it."

Now, I could finally take this old man's advice and try to open the car door, and it immediately unlocked. I shook my head in disbelief that it actually worked with this car. I said, "So I found my car that I drove here but what happens now? If there isn't anything wrong with the car ... then there must be something wrong with me!"

I checked my mirror to see if I was bleeding. But when I looked in the left side mirror, I could not for the life of me see my own reflection but one of a brown-haired, brown-eyed boy in my place. He looked to be my age and nothing like me at all and dressed like he came straight out of a thrift store, which for me, is something that I would never wear. *No...No... this can't be me, can it?*

I then started to make silly faces in the mirror to see if this truly was me, but I quickly noticed that he was doing exactly the same. *This cannot be real because none of this makes any sense. This must be some weird lucid dream, I guess, because that explains the green fog.*

But I didn't know about my answer to that because when I took a closer look at "his" shirt, it just didn't explain why my outfit had to change too. A couple of obvious signs are that I would never...ever wear a nice button-down shirt for my first day of school, but most importantly, my phone was gone! I desperately tried to look for it in all of my pockets and the back seat, where I distinctly remember tossing it to.

Finally, my grandpa's letterman jacket was missing somehow, even though I wore it while driving through the fog. *Oh man, my mom is going to kill me when I come back home without the jacket. I just gotta stay calm for now and head into school.* But I couldn't get my head straight about what I saw in the mirror reflection of that brown-haired kid. I wanted to find out more about him, but for now, I had to try my hardest to ignore that question in my head, for I had other things to worry about, such as school, especially before the bell rings. So, with that, I grabbed my backpack, which seemed and felt different too, but whatever, and headed to my school.

Chapter 3

Grand Entrance

Walking through that big wooden door, my senses were immediately signaling that I shouldn't be there, because why on earth would my school hang a big yellow banner for all the world to see that says "Welcome, Adams Highschool Class of 1960"? That isn't even the name of my school.

Now, this has got to be some dream. I mean, what's next? A crazy killer with a hatchet sneaking up from behind and killing me? I would expect something like that, but not some cheerleader handing me a flyer. Oh, and get this, the cheerleader didn't even have my school logo or letters either. Instead, there was some cougar on it with the words, *CA*. The cheerleaders were standing on opposite sides with each other passing out these flyers to students who walked past them.

I didn't even say anything to her. She just decided to run from behind and say, "Hey! Kid! Don't think we forgot about you," as she tapped my shoulder. I immediately turned around in shock, and she handed me a flyer. But the way she looked at me, though, as she handed it to me, creeped me out.

I don't know about you, but I totally got this weird vibe from her, like 'What are you doing here' kind of vibe, you know? Anyway, I just rolled my eyes at her and asked, "What the heck is this?"

She replied, "Sorry if I scared you. I didn't mean to, and this is our school flyer, and it's pretty important, so you better read it." She then took off somewhere, probably to meet up with her fellow cheerleaders.

I looked at the flyer, and there was nothing special about it. It just said something like, "Do you like to hang out and drink some delicious smoothies? Well, come on down to Pete's dinner today right after school, where you will have a great time and meet new people. Don't forget to say that you were sent by the Cougar Cheerleaders at Adams Highschool, where you will get 2 cents off when you purchase anything from Pete's Dinner by August 31st, 1959."

Wait, Pete's Dinner? There's no such thing or place as Pete's dinner or any dinner at all that I'm aware of where I'm from. Where or when exactly am I really because I never heard or been to this place called Pete's dinner before. When I finished reading the flyer, someone yanked it right in front of me. By someone, I meant the same blond cheerleader who gave it to me. I was not expecting her of all people to do this to me, and she had the courage to get right in front of my face just to say to me, "Hey, what are you doing here in our school? because I know every face of every kid in this town, and I haven't seen the likes of you before."

As I was about to say no, she stopped and said, "You must be Gary Walter, whose family is from California, right?" *Umm yeah, totally, let's go with that*, so I nodded. She then replied, "Great. By the way, you are so lucky to have a Boss Father."

"Yeah, I guess my dad is pretty great," I said.

"Only pretty great?" As she looks at me in disbelief. She quickly laughed it off, saying: "But I guess you get that a lot, dontcha'?"

"Oh yeah, all the time."

She tilted her head and replied, "Oh, I had no idea. I'm sorry."

"It's fine," I stated.

She quickly changed the subject. "I love your new ride, by the way."

"How did you--"

She interrupted me and said, "I saw you driving to school, and it's easy to tell you're a new kid when you're the only one who has California plates. That's something you might want to change while you are here. Also, I should introduce myself. My name is Janet Smith."

"Oh, it's a pleasure to meet you, Janet," I replied

Now, where have I heard that name before? Like I'd heard her name from somewhere, but I don't exactly remember where or when. I thought I actually said that out loud to her, but I didn't, thank goodness. But I actually said, "You know, I just realized who you look like!"

"Folks around here always say that I look like Marilyn Monroe."

"No, you kind of, uh, look like my grandmother, to be honest."

Soon as I said that, it clicked that this tough lady was my grandmother.

No way! While I was happy figuring out who this lady was and why I knew her, Janet, who still had no idea ... was not! She was so red in the face that it was the color of a bright red apple, I swear. She was so angry she slapped me so hard in the face that I still had the mark throughout the day.

Janet then said, "If you're done, let me show you around here, new kid, and even though you are a senior like one of us, we won't haze you as much, I promise." She then showed me classes that I had never seen before. As I'm walking around these hallways, I look in every classroom, and it's super obvious to me which room is for each subject.

Everything in the classroom looks totally retrofitted. I am talking about the chalkboards, old desks, especially the old school mascot, which is apparently a Cougar that I see roaming through the hallways every once in a while. It's so strange to me seeing everyone, especially myself, in retro clothing. It's just a shame this whole thing is not real, but one of my crazy-feels-real kind of dreams, and it would only be a memory by the time I wake up today.

While Janet is showing me around, she gets this bright idea that I must share "my" schedule with her. Even though she asked nicely, I asked why. She laughed and said, "Why? Isn't it obvious? I want to see what classes we have together."

I replied, "Oh," as I grabbed the supposed schedule out of my backpack, and as I looked inside, a paper with a name really popped out to me, and it said, "Gary Benjamin Walter." I didn't get a real good look until later, but it totally appeared out of nowhere. "Uhhh, here you go."

She then looked at it and said, "Thanks, and hey, we have English, Math, and lunch together. that's bad, especially English."

"Why is English so bad?" I asked curiously.

"Our teacher is so nice and very resourceful and he is especially resourceful for a new kid like yourself and he may seem terrible at first, but sooner or later, you'll like him."

That's when I heard this loud old school bell rang, and she stated, "Oh, that's the bell. let's go to the first period...come on, Gary."

We then took the stairs and started to head to English, which is on the third floor, by the way, and we were only on the first floor! I was so not having it today because I was totally sleep deprived at the moment, probably because I stupidly stayed up till 1 a.m. playing Fortnite with my friends, and I just needed a moment to rest. But that moment of peace just never showed up.

Chapter 4

The New Kid

As we were taking the stairs to my new English class, I admit being stuck for the time being wasn't as bad as I thought it would. But it was mostly thanks to my Grandma, who distracted me by just chatting and asking away about me. Plus, telling a little bit about herself, too, if I might add. I didn't really push for details about her because I knew all about her. But she wanted to know everything about me instead since, after all, I am the "New Kid."

The questions she asked were personal...almost too personal if you ask me. She starts off slow by asking me, "What do you think of the school so far?⊠" Not a bad question at first, so I answered, "I think it's great, but that may change throughout the day." Then she decides to throw this curveball question at me like, "How many siblings do you have?"

How am I supposed to answer that if my dream younger version of my Grandma doesn't even remember? Now, I'm starting to think maybe this is some weird reality after all. I lied and told her that I had two siblings just to get that question done and out of the way. I'm totally being honest with you guys right now and telling you I was so annoyed by my own grandmother at first because one, I didn't know that she acted like this before, and two, do I just tell her the truth and be done and over with of who I really am or not...since this is a dream after all? I then decided to just lie to her from now on. It made things so much easier for me.

But before she even had a chance to ask any more ridiculous questions, we made it to our English class. Before we even made it to the door, I stopped dead in my tracks because I had never switched schools before, unlike some people, and I didn't know what to do or say just in case this wasn't a dream but real. Janet, for whatever reason, decided to push me inside the classroom.

"Hey! Why did you do...ohhh--" I stopped talking immediately and just stared awkwardly as everyone was staring right at me as they were sitting in their seats.

I looked down and tried to find an empty seat, but I couldn't help but notice Janet talking to some guy at his desk. This guy got up, walked past me, kind of hit me in the shoulder, and just sat across the other side of the classroom. Janet then said, "Gary... come on and sit here before Ronnie changes his mind." I nodded and sat where this Ronnie kid used to sit.

You know what I just noticed? As soon as Janet entered the classroom, everyone was happy to see her, but as soon as I did, though, everybody was giving me the cold shoulder that Janet gave me earlier, which wasn't a good sign, but I just ignored all the dirty looks and cold stares.

This day just couldn't get any better for me because now, Janet wants to sit next to me. This is getting crazier and weirder by the minute. One second, she hates my guts, and now she wants to sit next to me in class. Just sitting next to her, let alone talking to her, feels like back in kindergarten, when my parents would spend a day with me in the classroom, but this is way worse. Sitting down at this desk felt like I was sitting on pins and needles, so I decided to take a closer look at the schedule that I saw earlier to distract myself from the pain. So, I opened my backpack and took a look at the schedule and was shocked to learn that Gary Walter is apparently a real person because why would a dream say a specific birthday for this guy, which was December 27th, 1941, while mine isn't even close to that date or season.

Also, the school he went to before coming here to Burrowsville, Michigan, was James W. Marshall High School in Los Angeles, California. Which is somewhere I've never visited or even heard of. The supposed dream that I am currently in is running on thin ice here, and I'm starting to think I am actually in 1959, but I'm still holding on to some hope, which is becoming less and less. With this new information in hand, I quietly kept it all to myself and just memorized the schedule of this "new" school the best I could.

When the old school bell finally rang, which seemed like forever, the teacher got up from wherever he was sitting and started to say the standard introduction that I'm all too familiar with. As he was introducing himself and what we would be learning throughout the year and blah, blah, blah, a kid who was to the right of me whispered to me in a menacing tone, "Just so you know, even though you're new doesn't mean you get the right to hit on Janet 'cause you know she's already going steady with someone...right?"

I whispered back, saying, "Well, I'm not trying to hit on her... what makes you say that?"

The kid replied, "The look on your eyes gives it away." But before I could answer back, the teacher caught me off-guard.

"Now, starting today and finishing tomorrow, each and every student here, including myself, will go, stand in the middle of the classroom and tell us a little about themself and what he or she did this summer...Now, since Gary is the only new face that I see, for now, he'll gladly go first and tell us a little bit about himself and what he did this summer."

I was then signaled to get up, so I nervously got up from my seat and said to the class, "Hello ...my name is Gary ...Walter, and I'm new around here, as you can tell, and up until now I lived in Los Angeles California with my family. The one thing that I did this summer was...was drag racing with my friends."

The teacher asked, "What kind of ride did you drive in this drag race of yours with your friends?"

"Well...uh, you see, the ride that I drive is not really mine, so to say, it's...my father's but he kind of lets me borrow it."

The teacher then said, "Hmph, that is a very interesting summer, Gary, and I bet your father would love to hear more about it, especially the part where you were "borrowing" his ride right after school today. You may sit down now."

I nodded my head and headed back to my seat where Janet, who sat on my right side, whispered, "Nice going, kid, you got in trouble on the first day, and now you may never be driving a nice car like yours ever again."

The Teacher then began calling someone else up, which was so boring to watch and listen to. He then told us that we had homework. Like, who the heck gives homework on the first day of school?!!! To be fair, it was easy; it was just writing down one word of how you are feeling right now and why. But everyone would be sharing this once we were done with introducing ourselves tomorrow.

Sounds simple enough, and by the end of class, all of us students left the classroom and went our separate ways, at least up until lunch. As soon as lunch came around, I arrived at the cafeteria, and when I entered, I had no clue where I was going to even sit because one of my real friends would've called me over by now, but they weren't in sight. As I was walking around the cafeteria looking like a complete idiot, I heard my name or "Gary's name" being called over. I turned around to see who was calling me, and I was surprised it was Janet. She wanted to know if I wanted to come sit with them.

I obviously said "Yes" because I didn't want to sit alone or eat in the bathroom, so I followed Janet where she and her friends were sitting. As soon as I got there, I immediately told her, "Thanks for letting me sit here." She replied, "No problem. I don't want you to sit alone on the first day." She then started to introduce me to her big group of her friends, which were about 15 people. Her main group of friends was not as much as I first imagined, but hey, friends are friends, I guess. Her group consists of four boys, if you include her "steady" boyfriend, Henry.

Those are the only boys in her group while she had a lot of girls. Janet introduced me to all of them, even the boy group. The first thing that one of the girls asked me was, "Is what you said in English class really true?" Seriously, what is with these people? What I said was around two hours ago, and they should really move on, but I guess not. I tried to answer the questions the best I could, but I had to repeat the story that I told Janet, which was saying that I'm from Los Angeles, California, and we moved to Michigan because of my dad's work in the car business.

Every one of Janet's friends felt satisfied with my answer and didn't ask any more dumb questions and decided that I was totally cool enough to hang out with them, which I so desperately needed if I wanted to fit in. Shortly after being accepted in this new group of friends, the girls started to fill me in on their conversations and things that had happened before I came here, like how there's a new diner down the street and more stupid stuff like that.

As I was trying to listen and keep track of their conversations, it was just impossible, especially with them arguing with each other almost all the time, like one person said, "That's wrong. This place opened on June 12th, not August 15th ...what the heck are you talking about?" and so on and so on.

While they were busy arguing, I was thinking to myself, *Man ...this has to be the most boring boomer decade to be trapped in, and I hate to be the poor sucker that's stuck here.*

But as of now, I just cannot for the life of me stand all the constant chatter like do they have nothing better to do? I wanted to tell them to shut up, but I couldn't.... it's like someone wouldn't let me. But hearing them and everyone in the cafeteria doing it as well was stressing me out. I'm serious. I can hear every single kid in this school's annoying voice and tone as they chatter away about beef with friends or sports games that happened or are going to happen. It's almost as if the voices are circling around my head at full volume.

Now, I'm starting to see why my generation takes cell phones for granted, or else I'd end up like these folks. Ahhh, man, I'm starting to miss my reality already, especially my family when or wherever they might be. Just as I was thinking about them, Janet had to ruin my moment and said, "Have you not been paying attention at all, kid?"

I replied, "Was it something about going to the movies, right?"

"No, I was talking about how.... how--" she stops and sees some kid in a letterman jacket and says, "Oh, isn't he dreamy?"

"Who's that?" I asked. She said "Oh right...I forgot to tell you, that's my steady partner Henry.... Robinson, and he is our star quarterback."

I insisted that Janet should circle him if she finds him so dreamy as I laughed. But as I laughed, I thought about what I just said and why, but I brushed it off by convincing myself that their unknown slang or language was starting to rub off on me almost like a virus, and plus, this is only a dream and sayings like this don't usually make sense to anyone. She suddenly said, "Maybe someday I will, and you will never hear the end of it."

Right......but Henry decided to stop and drop by our lunch table and right away noticed me but didn't really point out and said, "Who's the fream, and what's he doing at our lunch table?"

I asked, "Who, me?"

Henry answered, "Ya... you kid...who are you, and what are you doing here at our table?"

"I'm Gary, and I'm new...my family came from California, and Janet was the one who invited me to this table."

"Oh really....so what's really bringing you here to Michigan? Is it the dolls or--"

I interrupted him and said, "Well, my daddy works in the car industry, and--"

"Well, well, did you hear that, fellas? Looks like we got ourselves a drag racer on our hands, and where is this new ride of yours, kid?"

"Oh, it's parked," I said as I looked outside the window, "right there, actually." I pointed to my car.

"What...that ride over there?" as he pointed to some rusty-looking 47 Hot Rod.

"No, it's actually the one right next to it."

Henry looked impressed and said, "I dig that ride, man. But first, I want to blow you off in a little drag race tonight at seven on the new highway on fifty-first street. You can't miss it. So, what do you say, New kid? have we got ourselves a deal?"

I said, "I think I can dig that," as we shook hands. Henry and his gang then left.

When they left, Janet screamed at me, "Are you crazy going against him? Now, who do you think you are?" Before I had a chance to say something back, the bell rang, and everyone, including me, started to head back to their classes. I'm just glad that this first day of school was almost done because so far, only three classes left to go until I leave and forget this first day of retro school for good.

Throughout the rest of the day of "school," I learned more about Gary than I did in class. For example, Gary takes classes that I would never take, like lots and lots of math classes. My guess is that he wants to be an accountant or something, which is the complete opposite of what I have in mind, and by the way, did I ever tell you that Henry, you know the one who challenged me, is my grandfather?

I tried to deny that Henry Robinson is my grandfather, but I couldn't help but notice my scary resemblance with him because seeing pictures that were once black and white now in color really make a difference, let me tell you. But still, I don't know what my grandmother saw in him because what I could gather about my Grandpa so far is that his younger self is a genuine, smart-aleck who's very competitive, unlike his older mature self, and is quite the bully.

How I found that out, you may ask. Well, I apparently have the same 8th-period Gym class and teacher with him! Lucky me, huh. I'm in class with a school bully, and it is, of course, gym. Henry didn't even hesitate to bully me when he tripped me during the first lap on the first day of school where our teacher Mr. Jones or mad-dog as he wants us to call him from now could see. Soon as we were done running, he took attendance.

After attendance, Mr. Jones then proceeded to tell us of all the units we will be doing in all of his classes and how we will have the special honor of doing everything in reverse, starting tomorrow, and that is my least favorite sport, basketball. I hate that sport. I was never even good. But before Mr. Jones could say any more about this unit, the bell rang, and that meant the first day of school was officially over, and I could finally go home to my era and not this "boomer" era.

But not before Mr. Jones had to dismiss us so we could go to the locker room and change before we went home. So, with that, all of us boys headed to the Men's locker room where we changed, and once everyone was ready, we headed home. I was more excited to go home than all these fellas because I wasn't from here ... or I should say "this time."

Outside the doors, I noticed that everybody was cheering as they were leaving school with their books in hand and getting into their cars. As I was trying to find my own, I noticed that there were tons of cars that I don't recall parked near me. I managed to find mine only because of the California plates. *Ha, take that, Janet.*

Chapter 5

A Ride Home

As I entered my car, the search for a way home began right where I left off, but a little different. Now, I was searching for any signs of the fog showing up, so I could leave this place and forget about this dude named Gary, once and for all. But my search for the fog was quickly becoming a failure because it became clear to me that it was a bright, shiny summer day with no clouds in sight.

So, there was no chance of a fog showing up randomly. You know, I tried everything to get its attention....I really did. Either by looking around every corner of my car to see if there was some secret button or just snapping my fingers, but nothing ever happened.

Then it hit me. If this indeed is a dream, I should try to wake myself up. I didn't know why I hadn't thought about that sooner. So, I did what any normal person would do in my situation and slammed my head against the steering wheel. I even tried to slap myself just to wake up. But no matter how hard I did, I didn't wake up.

So, after letting everything out--like my anger, happiness, and sadness for a short while, I was finally ready to calm down and try to come up with a plan of some sorts to figure out what to do next, like I'm obviously here to do something, but one thing I do know is that wherever I am, Gary's parents are probably worried sick about him, and I should try and find his or my way back to his house before I get into more serious trouble. I said to myself, "Well, at least this day can't get much worse for me."

I turned the car on and immediately backed out of the school parking lot and headed somewhere, anywhere but here, and left the school as fast as possible. But I slowed down in awe once I got to this downtown area. It looked so different but so cool, especially seeing all these little shops that I never heard of, and most of all, I saw all these men in suits and ties while the ladies wore dresses coming out of tall buildings. I even noticed a couple of ladies who had small children with them going from store to store; these moms didn't seem to be distracted by their phone and let them roam free or let their kids be entertained on an iPad or phone, unlike a few mothers I know.

Driving through the downtown area was fun. *I gotta visit this downtown more in my free time, but I have somewhere to be,* so I turned on the radio and listened to some 50s tunes to help me get there, and it was great. Driving around sure is fun and all, but I asked myself what I was going to do next.

Soon as I left the downtown area, I decided to turn into the first secluded neighborhood I saw, where hopefully someone would let me stay for the night. That, or park somewhere and think and talk freely to myself about what to do next without being seen as a lunatic. When I got to a neighborhood that I thought was secluded, it actually wasn't because I could see and hear children playing outside with what looked like toy guns and laughing.

I knew I couldn't park at some random house with children around to see me talking to myself, so I kept driving until I either reached a dead end or didn't hear and see anyone. After driving straight for what felt like an hour, I finally saw no one outside. So, I gave myself the "all clear" and talked to myself, which I hadn't done since I left the school. I turned the car right to the side of someone's driveway, put it in 'park,' turned the car off, and said, "Phew! I Made it. Now, how am I going to get to Gary's house without using Google Maps or maybe ask around for directions?"

Then I got an idea and smirkingly thought, Oh, I don't need a map. I got his driver's license!

I immediately grabbed my wallet and opened it up to see his driver's license, but when I looked inside, it said My Name! My....name and address. I was shocked, to say the least, and even wondered how in the world this was possible. How could I see my own wallet when I wasn't even born in this era?! "Wait, what if...." I then grabbed my wallet and opened it up again, aimed it at the mirror, and it showed a mirrored Gary's address with his photo.

I said, "Now that's better, so it looks like I'm supposed to head to Franklin Street, and the house number should be number 508." I looked to see what street I was on, and I was apparently on Franklin Street and looked to the right to see the house number that I parked, and the house number just happened to be 436. This means if I just keep on going a little further, I should be able to spot his house. I immediately started my car, backed out, and continued driving.

Just when I was about to reach a dead-end, I spotted Gary's house number. I parked my car on the driveway, grabbed my bag, turned the car off, and slowly started to ring the doorbell to see if anyone was home as I did not want to try my key ring to open the door just in case someone was not home unless I absolutely needed to. As I am waiting for someone to open the door for me to let me in, I notice that this house is not like my house at all, especially when it's big and has lots of red bricks. All of a sudden, I see the door suddenly swing wide open with this tall older gentleman, and the first thing he said to me with an angry look on his face was, "Couch...now!" and pointed inside.

This guy is probably Gary's dad or my dad now, and he seems to be very mad at Gary, Aka Me! When he spoke, I felt like the entire room shook, especially when I got inside and sat down on this couch where he went full angry parent mode on me and said, "Gary, I'm very disappointed in you because I received a telephone call from your English teacher this morning and he told me how you had a blast this summer about some drag race with your friends and how I kindly "lent" you my ride to do such a thing. So, from now on until I see some responsibility in you, young man, I don't want you near my dealership again. You hear me?!"

I don't know why, but I said, "Yes, dad. I hear you loud and clear."

"Good. Now, how many times did you take my car out for a little joy ride of yours? How many times?" He demanded.

I immediately burst out, saying, "It was only 2 or 3 times, I swear."

"Hmph...but next time, if you ever get the chance to drag race with your buddies again, ask because I do not want you racing my rides all willy nilly, especially when these rides are meant to be sold to the hardworking American class. Hand over your keys."

"W-w-what...why?" I asked.

Gary's father simply said, "Don't make me say it again." With that, I was kinda forced to give him my keys, but I really didn't want to because it wasn't even my fault, to begin with.

When I handed him my car keys, I felt so defeated, but Gary's dad wasn't done lecturing me just yet and continued to ramble on, saying, "Thank you. Now, I don't want to hear any more complaints from any teacher about this. Got it? And don't you even think about drag racing my or your ride again because you are not going anywhere for the time being until I see some maturity from this childish antic of yours. So, for now, you will have to walk to school like how I did. Go to your room, Gary Benjamin Walter now!!!"

I said, "But it--"

Gary's dad interrupted me and replied, "Now!" and he really meant it.

Chapter 6

Grounded

So, I got up from the couch and marched to the left of this very long hallway, where I had to try and find my room without any help whatsoever. Somehow, I managed to find Gary's room only because it was the only Dark Green colored room throughout the whole house. I only found it because I had almost opened every single door of this house. But before I could even enter my room, something strange caught my eye at the end of the hallway. I walked away just as my hand was on the knob and headed down the hall. What I found to be strange was actually just an old framed family photo standing perfectly still on a table, almost like an elf on a shelf.

There was nothing special about the photo either, just three kids, especially one boy, one girl standing right next to each other, one taller than the other. Now those two were standing in front of a fireplace. But there's one little girl who was in front of the two kids that was **all alone**. She **wasn't** really alone, though, as she had two older siblings who were standing right behind her. What made this photo stand out from all the rest of the photos in this hallway is how I felt **drawn** to it, somehow like I could hear the children's distinct laughter and voices calling out to me. I don't know why I felt so drawn to it. I mean, it was just a family photo after all ...maybe there was something more to it, but I guess we'll never know the **real reason.**

As I took the framed photo from the table to analyze it more, I couldn't help but laugh to myself quietly at how much this little boy resembled Gary; it was almost like looking at a mirror. Then it clicked for me that this wasn't just a resemblance or a weird coincidence, but the little boy was Gary, so the two girls must be his sisters. This **must** mean that Gary is the middle child of this family.... Great.

I put the framed photo back on the table and looked at it one last time before leaving and heading back to Gary's room. When I got to his door, I slowly opened it and took a peek inside but couldn't see anything at first other than a silhouette of a bed and closet, but when I turned the lights on, his whole room just illuminated. I could now see everything from his radio clock on his nightstand to the old metal cars and trucks on his shelf.

As I'm messing around with his drawers looking for something....anything to keep my mind off from being "grounded,"

I found what appeared to be a rolled-up magazine or comic books. So, without thinking, I unrolled it and noticed that it wasn't either, but instead, an adult magazine. How did he even get a hold of this? But without skipping a beat, I rolled it back up and stuffed it back where I found it, ran and closed the door so nobody could see me looking or reading it so as not to get into more trouble. After that little scare, I was so beat that I just laid on the bed with the most purely exhausted look on my face but laying on that bed felt like I was laying on a rock.

While figuring out how to get comfy on this bed, I heard my door creak open, and when I looked, I saw this little girl with pigtails appear out of nowhere. I was shocked for a second but quickly figured out that this must be the little girl in that photo I saw earlier, and she was not a little girl anymore. She looked way older than she did in the photo now. Maybe aged four or five. But all I could say to her at that moment was, "What do you want?"

"Nothing really, other than to let you know that mom told me to come get you from your room cause dinner's ready."

"Great. I'll be there, just give me a minute, will ya? There's something I need to take care of real quick," as I closed the door on her. The main reason I did that to her was to walk around the room and decide right here, right now, whether or not I should leave this place and find the fog on my own by climbing out of the bedroom window or just suffer the consequences by talking to strangers who consider me "**family**."

I thought about it for a while and decided that *you know what... I made it this far without messing up Gary's life too badly, so why give up now?* With this thought in mind, I opened the door and exited with confidence as I headed to the unknown, where my fake family currently resided in the dining room **waiting** for me.

Chapter 7

Dinner

I followed this little girl all the way to the dining room, and when I arrived at the table, I saw all of his family members just sitting there chatting away, but they all stopped once they saw me walk in and just oddly stared down at me. It almost seemed like they wanted me to say something back to them or maybe say sorry for what I did or maybe why I was so late, but I never said a word to any of them. I just sat down at the only empty chair that was next to my....mother, I think.

As soon as I sat down, his family kept talking as if everything was normal, and from what I overheard, they didn't seem to mind that I was gone, which was a little concerning since I almost decided to ditch them. Anyway, Gary's mother cut the chatter amongst the family and said, "Thank you, Gary, for finally joining us for dinner, and since you were the last one to sit down, you know what that means. You'll have the honor to start us off with Grace."

I thought, *Grace ... Grace, what in the world is Grace?* Come on, brain, work with me here and... Aha I got it! Grace is the prayer that we say before eating, like what me and my family do before eating some lovely Turkey for Thanksgiving. I nodded and said, "Let's give thanks to God for the weather and the opportunity that God has given us here in Michigan. Amen." The rest of the family said amen, and my older sister whispered to me, who was the one that I thought was my mother, "That was a good prayer." Now, I don't know if she was being sarcastic with that comment or not, but I didn't care. I was starving!

As soon as I got handed a plate of something that looked straight out of a horror middle school lunch menu, I picked at what looked like mashed potatoes with gravy at the bottom. As I was picking at it more, Gary's mother said, "Gary, stop picking your food and eat it before it gets cold." With that, I had no choice but to have a bite of whatever this was supposed to be, and the smell didn't help at all. But as I took a bite, I was surprised that it tasted so good. Even now, I miss eating like that from time to time.

But anyway, while I was enjoying eating in peace, Gary's father just had to kill the mood and ask questions to "Mary" and "Susan," who are my sisters and just going on this rant about their day, etc. Like how Janet was to me. The conversation was just going back and forth with no sign of ever ending until I foolishly looked at him while I was eating. Gary's mom must have seen this and thought that I was simply being left out of the conversation because I saw her whisper something about me to Gary's father. He immediately stopped what he was doing and then started asking me how my day was other than my car being taken away.

Before I said anything, let me tell you that when I was younger, I hated the spotlight...hated it! I wanted nothing to do with the spotlight at all, even going as far as making and talking nonsense to people. One thing is for sure, though, that I never did say or do this to any family of my time-traveling adventure or in general. I guess you can say I grew up since then, but I'm just glad now that I'm older and much wiser now to see just how much of a self-centered jerk I really was. But enough about me, let's get back to the story, shall we...? so, where was I again?

Oh yeah, so this family was the first family, which you'll see later on that I really considered my second family. Sure, this was a rocky start, but I have a feeling that I'll get used to them and their antics in all good time.

I guess you can say it kinda felt like home. So, with me being comfortable enough with them already as they seemed non-threatening to me, I said, "It was a blast. I got shown around the new school and--"

Gary's mom interrupted me and asked, "Was it by a teacher or the principal?"

"No, it was just some doll, she was very nice to me and..." what? As I look around the dinner table, I see the whole family widen their eyes in shock like this boy never talked to a girl his whole life.

This was when I realized that oh ... this just got complicated. So, if I learned anything from the movies, I was going to have to try my best to be Gary, or else I may just get the boot. While I was thinking about how I was going to pull this off, Mary, who was to my right, asked, "Did she show any signs?"

"Signs of what?" I asked.

"Uhh, signs of liking you, kid," she replied.

"Maybe, I don't know. I wasn't paying attention. She was just showing me the new school."

She rolled her eyes at me and replied, "Well, the next time--if she ever decides to talk to you again--make sure you look for it, ok, and we will talk more about this later."

Gary's dad, who actually turned out to be impressed by me having contact with a girl for the first time other than family, said, "Well, Mr. Romeo! You will get your ride soon if you keep this up, even tomorrow maybe if you can get a girl or her phone number by dinnertime tomorrow."

Mary said, "Dad, that will never happen to him."

"Hmm, I don't know about that, Mare. Love does work in strange ways, like how I met your mother--that was strange," Dad replied.

Ok, on that note, I think I lost my appetite, but I couldn't pass up the opportunity to have dessert, so I ate this delicious slice of carrot cake that I somehow managed to eat without getting sick to my stomach. After dinner/dessert was over, I put my plate on the kitchen counter and headed to "my" room, where I should be able to finish the one and only homework assignment that I had. I'll **never forget** it. That one-worded homework assignment didn't take me too long for obvious reasons, and the word I chose was dull because that's how I felt right now writing this **simple,** boring word.

Chapter 8

The Talk

As soon as I was done writing, Mary barged into my room, saying, "Gary, here is the talk that you have been just dying for.... you ready? Do you remember the water incident on September 24th, 1947, in kindergarten?"

I quickly thought, *Oh how am I going to get this one right?* so I blindly said, "Uhh...... don't remind me."

Mary gave me this devilish smile and proclaimed, "I will happily remind you until the day I see you get a phone number written down of some girl or actually see her myself. I remember this day very well, in fact unlike you.

On that day, I was in first grade, and during recess, I saw you about to confront a girl that you apparently liked, but you didn't say a word to her; you just ran away crying because you peed your pants, and I had to say 'don't worry it's water' to everyone in the school while I knew it wasn't water--"

I interrupted her little backstory and complained. "Are you done? because I am."

But as I got up from my chair to leave, she stopped me and replied, "Ohhhh...Cut...the gas. I'm almost done...so, sit back down on that chair and let me finish my story, please!"

"Fine, carry on," was all I could say as I sat back down. She continued by saying, "Thank you. Now, where was I? Oh yeah, you didn't say a word to her or anyone for that matter for the rest of that school day or when mom picked us up, but when we got back home, you ran to your room crying, where I had to explain the news to Mom and Daddy once he got home about your little accident. Now, I'm pretty sure you know the end of that story.

Now, this is why we need to have the talk again because this is your last chance to get yourself a girl because it only gets harder after high school. Plus, if you find someone, you won't have any worries about finding someone to hang out with, not to mention having a dancing partner for the first time! So, the first thing you need to know on how a girl notices, my dear little brother, is..... Hey!!! Hey!" She then began to snap her fingers at me so I could pay attention or something. Or the fact that I almost fell asleep from her boring motivational speech.

Mary said to me, "Don't eyeball around. this is important because you don't want Mom or especially Daddy to explain it to you, do you?" I replied, "Uhh, no, Not really!"

"Good. So the first thing you need to know about how to notice if a girl likes you, little brother, is that you first have to be comfortable being alone with her, and I know for a fact that this part will be hard for you. Number Two, talk from the heart. Girls like myself always want a man who speaks his mind. Number three…. Make. Her. Laugh! This part is the easiest coming from you.

Finally, you are not going to like this one, but it's flirting. Don't be like a bum and do nothing but say something to her, Gary, and if you ask, I don't know how guys flirt, but it sounds pretty dreamy. Also, make plans for yourself. Go see a flick or go to a roller rink with the girl, perhaps. There's plenty of stuff to do around this town of Michigan than you may think. But I know what you're gonna say, and even though we aren't in Los Angeles anymore, we gotta make do of what God has offered to Daddy and us. This is for your own good, and I hope this is the final time I have this talk with you!"

She suddenly stomps out my room and closes the door. I immediately wiped my forehead in relief, and just when I thought the coast was clear from that awkward conversation, I said, "What a relief it's over!" But little did I know Mary was outside my room, and she responded. "I heard that!" After this, I think I had enough family and sibling drama for one day and got ready for bed.

But not before saying to myself quietly before drifting off to sleep, "Man, what….a….day, but even though this is not a dream, I just wish I can be back home…and sleep in a real bed, not this fake one, but I'll do anything to get back to my friends and family." With this, I slowly drift away to sleep.

Chapter 9

Morning Sunshine

Morning hits, and I wake up not to the sound of my stargaze alarm on my phone but to the sound of an old alarm clock ringing. Without thinking, I reached for my phone, but as I tried to grab it from the right side of my bed, I realized that my nightstand isn't where it should be, and I'm literally grabbing nothing but air.

Wait a second, am I still here? I then began to scan every corner of this room and said "Yep!" and "Welp I got to start my day somehow, and it's only 7:40 a.m...wait, I'm going to be late for school. Why did the alarm clock wake me up this La....you know what? I don't care. I'm a senior. I'll just show up at 8:25 a.m. or later. On that note, I got up from bed and made it, as usual, then started my day.

But for some reason, I decided to get dressed before eating some breakfast. So, I walked over and opened my closet, and that's when I noticed all these strange-looking clothes, especially a lot of plaid and polo shirts. I muttered, "Ok, let's have a look at what we're dealing with here."

Scrolling through the Clothes, "Jackets, Plaid, Plaid... Polo.... ugh, where does he keep the t-shirts?! But I guess this red plaid shirt will have to do for now." I then grabbed the red plaid short-sleeved shirt and put it on. I looked in the mirror to see how good it looked, and as soon as I did, Gary scared me. I said to myself, "Seriously, I got scared of.... my own reflection," with a sigh of defeat. "...Now, where are those jeans?"

As I tried looking for them desperately in the drawer with all my pants, they weren't there. He only had dress pants of almost every color. "I guess these red dress pants will do for the time being," I concluded.

As I tucked in this plaid shirt, I looked for a belt that kinda went with the look I was going for, and when I did, I looked in the mirror again to see the finished project, and this outfit looks so ridiculous but whatever. I then grabbed myself his watch, which was conveniently on his desk, so I could have something to keep myself occupied while walking to school. But before I had breakfast, I decided to go brush my teeth and comb my hair first because I had a lot of walking to do and could use the energy.

When I got to the bathroom, I decided to knock first because I didn't want any family drama like there was yesterday. Thank goodness I knocked because I heard someone say, "Occupied."

"Well, can you hurry up, please? I got school to go to."

The voice said, "Oh, Fine, but make it quick. I also have places to be." I opened the door and was surprised to learn that I was talking to Mary that entire time. She was busy doing her hair or whatever girls do in the bathroom to get ready.

Without any hesitation, I brushed my teeth and combed my hair as quickly as possible. But soon as I put the comb down, Mary said, "Ok, now that you are done, put an egg in your shoe and beat it." But before I could say one word to her, she was pushing me out the door. Once I was outside the bathroom, she slammed the door right in my face. So, this is what having an older sibling is like ...huh?

All of a sudden, I heard Gary's mom say, "Breakfast is ready, so come and get it before it's cold." I immediately headed down the hallway to the kitchen to go check it out. That's when I saw Gary's mom making some double stack pancakes for all of us. I thought *Pancakes...oh I love pancakes...I wonder how good they are.* I sat down in the chair that was closest to me in the kitchen.

While sitting down, I saw her put some pancakes on a plate, and they smelled like sweet, pure gold. I was so jealous for two reasons only. One is what kind of secret ingredient she uses for the pancakes, and two, how she even made a two-stack pancake look like child's play because I wanted to know. But even though

I was amazed...and still am, didn't mean that I was going to make it to school.

Gary's mom finally spotted me and said, "Glad someone's awake...Morning, Sunshine, and since you're the first one to be at the table, you know what that means. You get the honors of having my famous pancake with some nice crispy bacon on the side just the way you like it. Enjoy!" as she smiled. I yawned. "Good Morning. I can't wait."

Gary's mother then finished flipping the last pancake where she served me her "famous" pancakes. But she first handed me a fork and knife then the plate with the two stack pancakes covered with maple syrup. I swear that I can smell them right now as I talk about them to you. I now see why those pancakes have been dubbed famous. As I took my first bite, Mary, who was the second one to arrive at the kitchen table, showed up, and I guess judging by the look on her face meant that she normally gets the luxury of eating the pancakes that momma made first.

So, the real Gary must have set his alarm clock earlier yesterday morning so today he could finally eat his mother's famous pancakes...clever! I gotta say he's missing out on these pancakes 'cause they are for sure delicious. When I finished the famous pancakes, I headed back to my room and grabbed my school bag, and told my family that I was going as I walked to school all **alone**.

Chapter 10

School Belles

Who knew walking in the great outdoors is a great way to explore the unknown? I decided to take a look at my watch, and it was exactly 8:15 a.m. That's great.....not that I totally want to skip the first period and have some fun, but I'm still in the neighborhood, and I can't take a detour through time since I can't drive out of here for the moment. But the one thing that I liked about walking, though, is how quiet it was outside. Almost too quiet if you ask me. But it didn't take me long before this quiet suburban area started to wake up.

Like just now, I saw a dude in a white uniform get out of this delivery truck and carry this basket of glass bottles of what appears to be milk walking towards a house, but as he got to the front door, he waved at me before knocking. I waved back to him, but man, the 50s were weird. Why is everyone so friendly to me. Geez, what did I even do to make them so friendly to me? Oh my gosh, just now, an elderly woman waved at me, and she told me, "Good morning, have a nice day."

I nodded my head and continued walking, trying to wipe that strange encounter from my mind, but every time I tried, there were more of these strangers, some old and some young, being friendly to me. The first time was fine, but now there are more of them trying to strike a conversation with me or even wave at me. The more they waved or talked to me, the more I felt paranoid and just wished they would leave me alone. But that all stopped once I got into the downtown area where there should be a crosswalk around, if my memory serves me right, which should lead me directly to the school. Then for the heck of it, I decided to look at my watch again and was kinda surprised that not that much time had passed. You know, being how peaceful it is outside, I never really had a chance to look around and enjoy not seeing or hearing people blast music from their cars as much, or walking around with earbud headphones.

There is so much more to experience here. After a couple more crosswalks and the occasional glances at businesses and people turning the closed sign of their stores to open, I saw the school. Yeah, the one where I wished I would never see again. But this time, I figured I would do something different. Rather than just ignoring what people are saying, I would listen to people's conversations while walking through the halls. Perhaps I could figure things out and possibly get some answers as to why exactly I was stuck here.

Did I get any answers that day? No. All because Janet decided that this was a good time to talk to me in the corner of a hallway. She just HAD to ask what happened to me yesterday. I had no choice but to bring her up to speed on everything. But I intentionally forgot to mention what I needed to do to get my ride back and why I needed hers or some other girl's phone number to get it. Janet then asked, "Ok...So how did you get here then, did someone drop you off or...?"

I said, "No, I just walked."

She replied, "Gary.... I'm being serious here. How did you get here?"

I told her that "I really walked here, it wasn't that hard, and besides, my pops won't let me drive his car, so I had no other choice." I hate to say it, but Mary's advice was working! If this indeed is a sign, it's an awkward one. Considering the fact that I may or may not get my first phone number from a girl who is also my grandmother, I bet Mary didn't think of that one, but hey, I gotta take what I can get, right?

So, I decided to ask Janet if she had any plans for the weekend. She said, "I do...actually. I'm going to see a flick with my friends...you know the ones that I introduced to you yesterday? Well, we are seeing a flick tomorrow night. We are still deciding, but are you interested in joining us anyway?"

"Sure...I have nothing else to do," I said.

"Great. I'll tell the gang, and by the way, I may or may not know someone that likes you who is going to be at the movies with us."

My eyes widened, and I kindly asked her, "Can you please tell me who this someone is?"

"Not yet....but first," she then grabbed her notebook from her backpack, opened the notebook, and wrote her phone number on it. The two things going through my mind right now is...*is she really doing this*, and *why does it have to be her, my grandmother of all people, to get my first phone number from?*

After she was done writing, I guess it was my turn. However, I had no idea what the phone number of this dude named Gary was, so I just wrote down a bunch of numbers that came to mind and hoped she never tried to call me.

But the way Janet looked at me, though, while giving me her phone number seemed strange. But it was even stranger how she sounded when she said, "Here you go......and call me when you get home.... well...see ya later, Alligator."

As she left, the only thing I could say back to her was, "In a while, crocodile." Like how did I know to say that? Just as I asked myself this question, the first-period bell rang.

So, Adams high school starts at 8:30 a.m., ... interesting. I don't remember how I got to my classroom, but somehow, I did. I was thinking this wasn't a bad start to the day. Maybe I could accomplish a whole lot more.

Chapter 11

Here Comes Trouble

You know what I said about accomplishing a whole lot more. Well, for the most part, I was wrong. The trouble all started for me when I was walking to my 4th-period Physics class, and that was when somebody tripped me, and all of my books and papers that I had in my hands fell all over the floor. I sighed and got on my knees to pick up everything. As I was grabbing my stuff, I heard an unfamiliar voice jokingly say, "Oh, I'm sorry about that, kid. It was an accident, I swear." Ya right, if it was an accident, they would help me.

Just when I thought this day couldn't get any worse, a beautiful girl with brown hair wearing a poodle skirt came to my aid. As she was helping me gather all of my books and papers. She asked me, "Are you alright?"

"Yeah.... I'm alright, just mad."

She then said, "Well, you better watch out for those two." As I turn around where she is pointing at, I then see two guys in letterman jackets walking while high-fiving each other. "Yeah, those two who tripped you are part of Henry's Possie," she said. "What did you do to make Henry lose his lid and call his posse on you?" That's when it dawned on me that it must have something to do with the drag race that was supposed to happen last night.

Now, this girl was too cute to tell the truth, so I lied and said, "I-I don't have the slightest clue, and once again, thank you for helping me out. Well, see you around, I guess," and I left. As I walked away, I couldn't help but think of why I didn't ask for her name. But whatever, another opportunity was wasted and headed to the 4th period.

This wasn't the last encounter with Henry and his posse, though -- I met the ringleader himself. Now, I didn't want Gary's reputation being hurt or ruined from my mistake of not showing up at the drag race. But I kinda had a feeling that the worst was about to come. As soon as the bell rang, ending the 7th period, I had no choice but to head to the 8th-period gym class where I knew Henry would be …waiting for me.

As I headed to my gym locker where we were supposed to be dressing today, Henry surprised me by giving me a hard push from behind. I banged my shoulder into the locker -- that will surely leave a mark. Henry shouted, "I waited for you, Gary…and you didn't show …now, why is that?"

"Hey, let's talk about this after school?" I pleaded.

"Yeah, I think we're done talking. Let's settle this after school. Meet me in the parking lot. Don't chicken out. Got it!?"

Whew, I just dodged a bullet. But not for long.

Chapter 12

Nothin' But Net

As soon as I got dressed, I headed to the gym. After Mr. Jones, my gym teacher, took attendance, he said to all of us, "We are going to be doing something different today. I want everyone to get into groups of two when I blow my whistle." All I could think was, *Oh great! Just please let me be paired up with anyone but Henry.*

Mr. Jones blew his whistle, and it was like a madhouse. I immediately tried to find somebody, anybody. But wherever I looked, there was already a group of two forming. All the while, Henry was just standing there, whistling away. Mr. Jones spotted me and shouted, "Walter, what are you doing standing around? Find a partner!"

"I-I-I can't find one," I stuttered.

Henry then walked up to us and said, "Don't worry, Mr. Jones. I'll be Walter's partner."

"Thank you, Robinson. Alright, Walter, your problem is solved. By the way, you two boys might want to cover your ears right now."

Screech, Beeeep!

"Alright, students," said Mr. Jones, "the reason why you are in groups of two today is because we are going to play a new game that I like to call Double Horse. Now, you probably have played something close to this back at home, but we are doing something different. I am going to assign you a team number, and you are going to face off with odds vs. evens.

The goal is simple... don't get a horse! But keep in mind this is only a game, but you're getting graded, so no cheating... I'm watching you, Robinson. If I see anyone else cheat, then both you and your partner are out of the game, and you get a zero for the day. Plus, I am gonna make you run laps for the rest of the period. Do I make myself clear?"

We all chorused, "Yes, sir!" Then Mr. Jones began to assign us team numbers by counting us off, "One, Two, Three." Just as he was assigning group 4, Henry hit my shoulder and said, "You better not mess this up for us, Gary."

Mr. Jones then got to us and said, 'You two are number five." We both nodded, and Mr. Jones moved on to the next group. When he finally finished counting the last team, he said, "Now that each team has a number, I will assign you a court to play on. If you lose the game, the losers need to move to the next court on the right. Winners stay put. Starting out on court one, we have…..five and six." We both nodded, and I volunteered to grab us a basketball. His instructions were all a bit fuzzy to me, so I asked, "Uh, how do we start the game?"

Henry said, "Well, I don't know what people in California do, but around here, chickens go last. Just then, he grabbed the ball from my hands and took the first shot. So, we go first." No big deal, right? But the only problem is that he never let me have the ball — ever. The only thing he did was wait out the clock and dominate the floor with his little jukes and shots while I just stood and watched the show.

As I was helplessly watching Henry beat one team after another, something extraordinary happened—he messed up. I mean, he completely messed up! All he had to make was a basic free throw. Now when the ball was floating in the air, it seemed like time went into slow motion. The basketball hit the rim twice. Once hitting the backboard and again hitting the left side of the rim, and then it fell to the ground — bang! It seemed like the whole gym echoed.

Everyone was shocked when he missed. All Henry could say to me was, "Don't mess up," as he passed the basketball to me hard into my chest. But before I made my shot, one of the members of team six named James said, "What are you talking about, Henry? It's not Gary's turn yet; it's mine since you missed. That's how the game works, remember?" James then grabbed the basketball from my hands.

James tried to make an easy layup with one hand, but he didn't even make it to the net. He tripped on his own two feet before he could even make the shot. We all laughed at him while he was getting back up on his feet. But he begged us to let him try again. We all said, "No way, you almost had it, but you missed." Finally, it was my turn—my time to shine.

After watching Henry dominating the court, it made me stop and think, "Now, what am I going to actually do?!" I decided to try something risky (or maybe even stupid), but I was going to try an old school with a signature basketball move that Michael Jordan once did. I'm not talking about a slam dunk because that would be too obvious. Not to mention obviously, I can't jump. But how about a 3-point shot from half-court? Now, that's something that no one had ever seen. The 3-point line wasn't even a rule in basketball yet. I took a deep breath and started to dribble towards the back court. I turned around at the center circle, and BAM, I took the shot. Everything went into slow-mode again. The ball was flying, and the jaws were dropping as it approached the rim—swoosh! The crowd went wild! ... well, actually, the crowd went silent.

Henry stood there in shock and asked, "Who-who taught you that?"

"Micheal Jordan," I replied very proudly.

"Who's that?" asked Henry. Oops! I messed up. I tried to recover by saying, "Micheal Jor--. He...uh, you don't know him. He was an old friend of mine back in California."

"Did he ever play on a basketball team? Because he sounds amazing," Henry asked.

"Yep, he sure is — he's the greatest."

Henry seemed to buy what I said, and so did everyone else who listened, so I guess using "the new kid logic" still worked, ha! Henry, who was still in shock, said to me, "We gotta talk about the shot you made later." But before we got back to our game, Mr. Jones blew his whistle and said, "Alright, everyone, form a line and tell me how many wins and losses your team has."

Henry and I got in line and were trying to remember our score. I said to him, "I think we beat five teams today."

Henry responded, "Yeah, I think you're right."

Then before Mr. Jones let us go, he said, "We'll continue playing on Monday, so remember who your opponents are."

We all headed towards the locker rooms. As I was walking to my locker, I just knew this wouldn't be over between Henry and me. Something bad was going to happen soon — I could feel it.

Chapter 13

A Close One

Well, that moment did happen, but I didn't expect it so soon. Just as I put in my locker combination to get my clothes, I felt a tight grip on my shoulder. I turned around, and it was Henry staring right at me.

"What do you want, Henry?" I begged.

"Oh, nothing. Nothing in particular. Let's just say I'm giving you a little reminder — in case you forgot! We're still meeting after school in the parking lot. Where we're gonna have a little chat about the drag race."

I told Henry, as I was still getting my dress pants on, "Just so you know, I didn't forget. I'll meet you there." Then Henry surprised me with a good comeback. "Oh, we are going right now. Finish up getting dressed. I'm going to follow you. No tricks this time. I have a feeling you would chicken out."

As I grabbed my backpack, Henry pushed me out of the locker room door. As we headed down the hallway, I thought how weird this whole situation was. Like, I was going to die at the hands of my own grandfather.

Once we were outside to, uh, "chat," Henry got in my face and shouted, "Well, well, here we are, Gary! So, what's your deal? Why didn't you show up? What are you, some CandyAss or somethin'?" Then Henry punched me in the gut super hard. I immediately fell to the ground, trying to catch my breath.

"No!" I shouted back. "I'm not a CandyAss! I would've loved to race my ride against your piece of junk any day, but my Pops took my ride away from me."

"Now, that's a lame excuse." Henry laughed. "So did the dog eat your homework, too?" he continued. "Well, I guess I should expect that from Mr. California. Around here, we do what we say we're gonna do." He was pounding his fists together.

But I'll tell you what. I'm gonna give a loser like you a break. "But you better get smart real quick. Don't be late the next time, or else," shouted Henry. Gulp! I have a feeling my luck is wearing off.

Chapter 14

Family Baggage

Soon as Henry left me alone, I ran straight home. Man, I couldn't believe I'm saying this, but I just wanted to get back to Gary's house. I knew I'd be safe there. Soon as I got to the driveway, I was surprised to see Mary in the window waiting for me. As soon as I walked up the steps, she opened the door slightly and asked, "Well, did my teaching work out for you?"

"Sure did, sis. Take a look."

I showed her the phone number, and apparently, that was the magic word. She then opened the door fully and let me in.

As I walked into the house and headed to my room to put my backpack away, I heard Mary from the hallway say, "If you're wondering where Mom is, she went to go get groceries and should be back about now." Just then, I heard the door open, and Gary's mom entered and said, "I'm back, and hey, Gary, can you be a gentleman and help bring the rest of the groceries in for me?"

I put my backpack down and headed outside, where I saw this long red station wagon on the driveway. I walked towards the rear of the car and opened the door, and saw like fifteen brown paper bags. Geez, these old cars are huge. One by one, I brought all the groceries in, and when I finally got to the last of the groceries, Gary's Father was surprised that I was outside and asked, "You're not trying to sneak out with the car.... are you?" I turned around slowly and said, "W-w-what no, I'm just helping Mom with the groceries. But actually, now that you mention it, I have something to tell you at dinner."

As soon as I headed back inside the house towards the kitchen, I announced, "I did it." Gary's mom thanked me and said, "Dinner will be ready at 5." I put the last of the groceries in the food pantry. Then Gary's Mom asked, "Before you go to your room, can you do one more thing for me?"

"Sure, what is it?"

"Could you please go downstairs in the basement and tell your sister Mary to come up here and help me prepare dinner?"

"Will do," I answered. Thinking to myself, *there's a downstairs? How do I get there? I assume there is a mystery door that leads to the basement around here.* I opened one hallway door -- which was a broom closet. Luckily, Gary's mom didn't see me because that would be hard to explain. I opened the next door, and there were the stairs.

Now, it seemed quite dark down there. There was just one light bulb above the stairs. I was thinking, this is how every horror movie starts. I tiptoed down the steps and saw Mary folding clothes on a big wooden table. She seemed to be humming a song to herself while doing her chores. I called out, "Mary," but she didn't hear me. So, this time, I shouted, "Mary!" She jumped and turned around to look.

"Geez, you startled me, Gary. What the heck do you want?"

"I'm just letting you know that mom wants you to go upstairs and help her prepare dinner," I answered

"You know you could've just told me that quietly. There was no need to shout."

"But where's the fun in that?" I asked.

Mary answered, "Oh, you think you're so clever. Here's something to laugh about." That was when she grabbed my arm and started to twist it harder. I said Owh...Owh...Uncle...Uncle! She let go of my arm and said Do that again and... I'll make sure to twist it even harder.

"Oh, I oughta..." I said to myself... Man she is starting to get on my nerves! I huffed and headed back upstairs through the kitchen and passing, I told Gary's mom that Mary was coming up soon, and after that, I headed straight for my room and just laid on my bed to relax because I definitely needed it after today. As I was staring at the ceiling, I thought, *I'm starting to get the hang of things here.*

Chapter 15

In the Driver's Seat

The rest of that day was **great**. I told Gary's dad that I got a **girl's number**. He was both **surprised** and **impressed** that it happened so quickly. As promised, he handed me my keys back and not a moment too soon. I had plans to see a movie with Janet and her friends that Saturday night. Around noon on Saturday, I called Janet to find out what theater we should meet at. Janet said that everyone was meeting at The Silver Fox theatre at 6 p.m. I finished my outdoor chores at home and took a shower to get cleaned up.

I was so happy to get my car back. I left home early just to cruise around for a while. As I drove towards the entrance, I realized that this wasn't a theatre at all. It was an outdoor drive-in. *This will be cool*, I thought. I'd heard of these before but never actually seen one -- let alone watched a movie from the driver's seat of a car before. I hope they have buttered popcorn. I saw Janet's car and managed to park just a few spots away. I turned my car off, got out of my car, closed the door, and headed toward Janet and her group of friends.

Janet spotted me walking towards them and said, "Hey Gary, glad you made it. We were just talking about you. I want you to meet my friend Catherine -- close friends call her Cathy," Janet said with a wink.

Just then, Cathy turned around, and our eyes met. That's when I said, "Hey, haven't we met before?"

She replied, "Yeah. I think we did."

"Right, you helped me pick up my books after Henry's posse ran into me in the hall."

Janet interrupted us and said, "Hey, the movie is about starting in five minutes, let's get something from concessions before the line gets too long."

As we walked towards the concession stand, I looked around and quickly realized that Janet set me and Cathy up on a blind date. Whoa, now I was getting nervous. How did Janet know that I liked this girl? Like, really liked her.

While we were in line, I looked at the menu board of prices for snacks and drinks that was hanging right above the concession counter, and before I ordered, I asked Cathy, "Hey do you want anything to drink or eat before the movie starts?" She said she'd just have a Coke. I asked, "Are you sure you don't want any popcorn with that? Because it's a movie experience without it."

She chuckled to herself and said, "Maybe at intermission."

When it was finally my turn, the old man behind the counter asked, "What do you want, son?"

"I'd like to have two bottles of Coke and one large bucket of buttered popcorn, please," I replied.

He looked at me funny and said, "Did you happen to bring a bucket and a cow with you? We only have one size bag of popcorn, and it comes salted." Well, so much for impressing my blind date. I laughed it off embarrassingly and replied, "Ha, ha... that's right, just the one bag of popcorn, please."

As we walked back to Janet and her friends sipping our drinks, Cathy asked me, "Hey, do you mind if I watch the movie in your car?" I nearly spit out my drink, thinking to myself that I must be dreaming. I replied with a resounding "YES! ... I mean, uh, yeah, sure. My ride is right over here."

As I opened the passenger door for her, she hopped right in and said, "Thanks." The movie that was playing tonight was North by Northwest, featuring Cary Grant. It's kinda like a James Bond movie. As we were watching the movie, Cathy seemed to like me and moved closer, and that's when I offered my bag of popcorn to her.

After the movie was over, Cathy said, "Thanks for the popcorn, Gary. We should do this again sometime...you know." As she was about to open the car door, I said, "Wait. Cathy...I was wondering, uh do you have any plans for next weekend?"

"No.... I don't think so?" she replied.

"Oh, maybe you and I could go to King Frosty's Ice Cream Parlor downtown? I... I could pick you up," she said.

"Ok .... Sounds like a date, then." I replied

"Yeah, I guess it is.... pick you up at 6?"

"Perfect," she said, gave me a kiss on the **cheek**, and bolted out the **door**.

I watched her skipping towards her friends. They all turned toward me and waved goodbye. As I waved back at them, somewhat in shock of what just happened, I thought to myself that this was not just a great day; it was a great life. Too bad it wasn't really my own.

Chapter 16

Whip Cream with a Cherry

For the rest of that night and all of school next week, I could not stop thinking about her. But I did manage to call Janet somehow during the week and asked her if she knew where Cathy lived, and she gladly replied. "Oh, she lives on Oak Park Ave, house number 237, and that's just a few blocks away from school … good luck."

I thanked her, hung up the phone, and thought of how in the world did she know about this date with Cathy. But you know what, that doesn't matter. I just know that this isn't a walk in the park, and I actually got to try and win her over for real this time. I just don't know how I'm going to do it.

This whole second date is making me sweat, and my hands are shaking just thinking about it. When the day finally came and me spending a ridiculous amount of time in my room preparing myself by talking in my room: "You can do this. It's just some doll ...girl...how hard can it really be?" I left the house early once more to try and find Cathy's house. After a few mins of driving around, I spotted her house, but before I even got parked, I checked my watch to see what time it was, and according to my watch, it was exactly 5:54 p.m. I figured that Cathy wouldn't mind if I showed up a few mins early, and this could be a good time for me to get to know her parents while I am at it.

So, I drove to her house and parked in the driveway, turned the car off, got out, closed the door, and began to call her by name while standing right at the front door. She opened the door and said, "Hi, Gary, it's so good to see you, but before we go, I want you to meet my parents, so come inside. Don't be shy."

I gulped and headed inside to stand right by the front door. That's when she said, "Hey Dad…...Mom….can you come here for a second? there's someone that I want you to meet." I then saw them both coming out of the kitchen and coming towards me.

"Mom...Dad...I would like you to meet my boyfriend, Gary."

I thought to myself, boyfriend….boyfriend? We are only on our second date, and by the time we get to the third, we'll probably be married.

Cathy's Dad started, "Oh, so you're the boy that my daughter can't stop talking about at the dinner table all week long, huh?"

I replied, "Yes, sir."

"So, what makes you so special from all the others?" he continued.

Cathy shrieked, "What are you saying, dad?"

"I'm only kidding. So where are you two kids heading out tonight?"

"We are only going to King Frosty's for some ice cream," I answered.

"Only that and nothing else?"

"No, sir, that's it," I clarified.

Cathy's dad grunted and said, "Just make sure you bring her back home by 9 p.m. sharp. Not a minute later, or this might be the last time you'll be taking her out. Remember to drive safe and slow. There's someone very dear to my heart that you'll be driving."

"Will do, sir," I replied.

As we headed to the car, Cathy murmured, "That went better than expected. Nice job, Gary." As we slowly pulled out of the driveway, we waved goodbye to her parents and headed towards King Frosty's Ice cream Parlor. It was a rather quiet drive for the first few blocks, so I decided to turn the radio on to break the silence.

While I was scrolling through the channels, Sea Cruise by Frankie Ford came on, and before I continued scrolling, Cathy said, "Stop. That's my favorite song!"

She then began to dance in her seat and shake her hair around. I remember watching old videos of Elvis fans going crazy. It was strange to see it in person.

Once we pulled into King Frosty's parking lot, it was almost full. There were people everywhere enjoying their ice cream on a warm September evening. I managed to get a nice spot near the entrance of the place. I turned the car off, got out, and walked around to open the passenger door for Cathy. Cathy said, "Gary, I just love this place. I've been coming here since I was a kid. I'm so glad you chose it."

"Really? This is actually my first time coming here," I replied.

"I bet you'll love it too. They have the best ice cream in town."

"Must be. Seems like the whole town is here."

When I first saw the ice cream parlor, I was shocked to see how cool everything looked. This was exactly how my grandmother Janet described it to me; she even got it down to the smallest detail. There were workers in white uniforms that had a yellow crown on the top right side. There were soda machines and lots of neon and chrome everywhere, just as she said.

It was our turn to order, but I wasn't ready, so I told Cathy to go first. She said, "I'll have one Hawaiian Sherbet ice cream in a waffle cone with whipped cream and a cherry on top, please."

The worker said, "Coming right up! So, what will you have?" as he looked at me.

"I'll have one banana strawberry ice cream in a waffle cone with whipped cream and a cherry on top, too." I then looked at Cathy, and she smiled back at me with a wink.

We got our ice cream and walked outside to sit on a bench together. I asked, "How's the Ice Cream?"

"Good...do you want to try?"

"Sure, and you can try mine too," I said.

"Ok."

I had a lick of hers, and wow, that was sour.

"What's wrong, you don't like it," she said.

I looked back at her and answered, "Well... I've never tasted anything like that before. What did you say this flavor was?"

"Hawaiian Sherbet," she replied.

"Oh, that's a taste I won't forget." Cathy continued to lick my ice cream.

"Hey, save some for me!" I protested. She laughed and gave me my ice cream cone back.

"Thanks for leaving me some."

"Something is better than nothing," she said.

"Yeah, I guess."

Cathy then asked, "So Gary, a little birdie told me that you're from California. Is that true?"

"Yep, the birdie was right. I'm from Los Angeles, California."

Cathy gasped and asked, "Thee Los Angeles, California?! I've always dreamed of living there. The sun, the ocean, the glamorous life. So what was it like living there?"

"Well, it was all that, but after a while, even the glamour gets boring."

"I don't think I would ever get bored of California," Cathy replied. "So, what made you move all the way here?"

Man, she asks tough questions. Now, how am I going to answer that? I guess I have to wing it.

So, I said, "I got two words to answer that....my dad. He got transferred here with his job."

'Yeah, that's tough having to make new friends and all."

"Yeah, making friends is tough, but apparently, making enemies is easy."

"Oh, you mean Henry and his posse. How's that going?" Cathy asked. Just then, we heard a loud car screeching its tires around the corner and saw it coming our way. It screeched as it stopped right in front of our bench. It was Henry and his gang.

Henry leans over and barks out his window, "Hey, loser….we are gonna do this or what?"

I shouted back, "Uh, now's not a good time. I'm kinda busy."

"There's never a good time with you, huh. You've been dodging me for days. We're racing tonight. Meet me by the new highway on fifty-first street; you can't miss it. See you there at 8:30."

Chapter 17

A Race for the Ages

I looked at my watch, and it was 7:30. That meant I only had one hour before I had to meet Henry and race him, but that doesn't give me enough time to drop Cathy off for her curfew.

So when Henry finally left us alone, I said with a sigh of defeat, "So much for our date now, huh. I guess I got to drop you off home now."

Cathy replied, "What...no! Gary, you're not dropping me off. I want to stay and see you race."

"But I don't know if I have enough time to drop you off home before we both get in trouble with your dad."

"Don't worry about my dad. I'll handle him. You just get ready for the race. I want to see you win."

When we arrived at the Highway, Henry said, "Glad you made it...now the race can start."

I replied, "Cathy, it's safer to watch the race from outside." She nodded, but before she got out of the car, she gave a kiss on the cheek and said, "Let Henry eat your dust."

I asked Henry, "So how are we starting the race?"

Henry said, "I'm feeling generous tonight, so why don't your girl line us up and drop the scarf?"

Cathy said, "Let's do this, boys."

Well, this is getting interesting. My car is a 1959 chevy impala with a small block v-8, and Henry has a 1957 Plymouth fury with a 350 v-8 with dual four-barrel carburetors. He has more horsepower than me, but my car has better transmission. Overall, our cars are pretty evenly matched, so it's going to be a matter of driver skill to win this race. Cathy stood at the starting line as we were revving our engines and pulling up. Henry said, "Alright, Gary...last chance to chicken out."

I shouted back, "Not a chance. I've been looking forward to this for a long time. By the way, did anyone tell you that you drive a grandpa car?"

"I'm going to make you eat those words, Gary," Henry said.

We each revved our engines and inched up closer to the starting line. Cathy held her arms out as we lined up our cars. Cath said, "Are you ready, boys? When I drop my scarf, you go."

My heart was racing, and I couldn't believe what was happening. I'm about to race my grandpa. If I screw up now, I'll never live it down. Cathy then took off her scarf and raised her hand, then I thought to myself, *This is it.*

Next thing I knew, Cathy drops her scarf, and I slammed my accelerator to the floor. Tires are screeching, the engines are roaring, and off we go into the distance with our tires smoking. Henry got the jump on me, but I was right beside him.

I shifted into second gear and started to pull away. I thought to myself, *Yes...this is it. I'm going to win.* I shifted into third gear, and I started to see Henry's headlights in my rearview mirror. I was so busy looking at my mirrors that I almost forgot where I was going. I looked over the hood and started to see smoke. Did I just blow my engine? Gary's dad will kill me. But as I looked closer, I saw that it wasn't engine smoke. This smoke had a greenish glow to it.

Wait, does this mean....no it can't be. What about Cathy? I still had to drive her home. What about Henry? Does this mean I won? What the heck is going on? All of a sudden, I realized that I wasn't even on the road anymore. There was no road, not even a finish line, and nobody anywhere. Why is this happening to me? Why now? I guess the fog still has plans for me. But where am I going next? I'll find out soon enough.

CPSIA information can be obtained
at www.ICGtesting.com
Printed in the USA
LVHW050310290321
682793LV00020B/2064